The ADVENTURES of Papa and Sunshine

To order additional copies of this book, contact:
Xlibris
844-714-8691
www.Xlibris.com
Orders@Xlibris.com

ISBN: Softcover   9781-6641-7792-5
         Hardcover   978-1-6641-7793-2
         EBook   978-1-6641-7791-8

Library of Congress Control Number: 2021911060

Print information available on the last page

Rev. date: 06/01/2021

The ADVENTURES of Papa and Sunshine

Kitoto sunshine Love

Beep, beep, beep, beep,
beep, beep! beep!

"Sunshine, Papa is out front!"

"OK, Mom," she yelled.

Papa always picked Sunshine up at
ten sharp every Saturday morning.

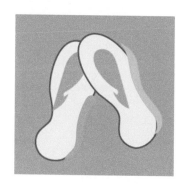

Sunshine, being the bright, boisterous seven-year-old little girl she was, always made sure to wear pink clogs for the occasion. It was a welcome break from her high-top sneakers, and easier to walk in, than her ballet slippers.

Papa loved this, because she could tap to the music while they danced down the street. Papa loved to sing songs from the showbiz years.

He relished educating her on a musical genre that had such an impact on the world, while he'd teach her how to sing.

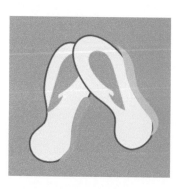

Papa pulled up on this Saturday morning to his old house in Sunnypark to pick up Sunshine. She lived in a historic part of town, where sidewalks were all brick or cobblestone and perfect for dancing.

Her parents named her Sunshine, after her smile. She arrived in the world as a "beautiful bouquet of joy," and Papa wanted the whole world to know it.

"Sunshine?"

"Papa!"

"Grab your umbrella, sweetheart,
we're going for a walk today."

"Where are we going?" "It's a surprise."

"Doo, doo, doo, da, da, doo, doo, doo, doo, doo doo doo doo, da da... 'Singing in the rain,
just singing in the rain, what a glorious feeling. I'm happy again.'"

"When were you ever sad?"

Papa smiled. "Those were Gene Kelly's
Feelings, sweetheart, not mine."

"Who was she?"

Papa laughed. His insides
shook, he grabbed his sides,
and he laughed and laughed
and laughed.

Afterward, as it happened every time,
he would end his laughter with a
quick little dance number.
Sometimes it was James Brown's
slide. Other times, it was a tap dance,
but Papa always had a dance inside.

Today, it was a quick tap in a puddle.

"Gene is a man. He's a dancer in Hollywood.

"Oh!" Sunshine's one-word response
had volumes in its deliverance.
"Oh, I had no idea a man could be named
Jean. Oh, Hollywood must be
where dancers come from." "Oh, the song
is from a musical."

"Can we go to Hollywood, Papa?"
"Of course we can. I would take you
anywhere."

"Anywhere?"
(Sang) "Anywhere for you."

Papa was a world-traveled musician
who knew a lot about so many things.
His knowledge and wisdom almost
matched his musical charm, but not quite.

Papa had written a hit song that
gave him adventure and a tour
with the most well-known music
band on the planet, but to
Sunshine, it was just another
cool thing about her dad.

Papa taught Sunshine "Singing in
the Rain," and soon she forgot
that she didn't know where she
was walking.

She traveled past her favorite fountain,
but because of the rain, she abstained
from jumping in today. Papa had
her so entertained she hardly noticed.

"There's the most beautiful girl in
the world."

Sunshine's reflection was smiling
back at her.

They had reached the store.

"Please come in."

A lovely brunette opened the door for them
and asked them to take their coats.

"A beautiful coat for my beautiful daughter!"

"Wow! Papa!"

Sunshine's eyes fixed on a red, green,
gold, and pink plaid coat with a pink ribbon tying
it all together about chin length. It had
a white faux fur collar and faux fur cuffs.

"We'll take size 6," Papa said.

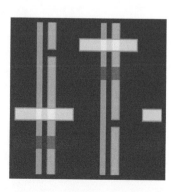

Twirling around in her new coat, Sunshine burst into the song "Hello Dolly." It was Papa's favorite, and it always made him smile with pride.

The store owner heard her and invited her to sing in his new commercial for his store.

Papa was so proud.

"Don't forget his name, sweetheart."

"Mr. Shreiv."

"That's it! I'm proud of you."

"Papa, can I wear my coat home?"

"I'm sorry, sweetheart, it will get wet in the rain. How about a piggyback ride, and we'll carry your new coat too?"

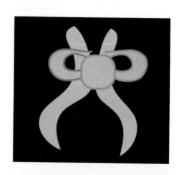

"Yay!"

Sunshine did a curtsy for Mr. Shreiv and his assistant and followed her father outside.

Carefully clutching her shopping bag, she jumped onto Papa's back, and he neighed like a horse.

Sunshine giggled. The ride home was fun. Papa skipped in puddles and sang to her as he galloped home.

"Arrived, little lady."

Sunshine giggled. That was, until she realized
she was home. Then she laughed and called for her mom.
"Mommy, look, Daddy's a horse!"

"I see that."

"Hi, Mom."

"Hi, Papa."

Sunshine giggled. She loved how her parents
called each other Mom and Papa.

"Sunshine has a surprise for you."

"I'm going to be on Mr. Shreiv's TV!"

"You mean his TV ad?"

"Yup, and his TV commercial too."

They both looked at each other and laughed.

Papa and Sunshine showed her mom
how to sing and dance in the rain.

"What did you buy for our daughter
this week?"

"Nothing too extravagant. Just the most
expensive coat they had. Only the best for
my best."

Mom laughed and twirled in the rain.

Sunshine giggled and splashed them.

Soon, it was time to go inside.

"Achoo!" Sunshine exclaimed.

"Oh, do you want to come inside
for some chamomile tea?"

"Yes, please."

So they all went inside, while Mom
fixed them some chamomile tea
and toast, and Papa poured the tea.

Sunshine's commercial for Mr. Shriev
was next Saturday, but that's
another story.

Printed in the United States
by Baker & Taylor Publisher Services